# DOG STORY

## by Kathy Henderson

## illustrated by

## Brita Granström

BLOOMSBURY
CHILDREN'S
BOOKS

Jo wanted a dog more than anything else in the whole wide world.

Her parents' hair stood up in the air.

'Imagine the mess!'

'Imagine the bother!'

'No,' said her mother.

'No,' said her father.

'But if you're very, very good we could get a neat little mouse in a neat little cage.'

So off they went to the pet shop and chose
a little brown mouse with a wiggly pink nose
and a long bootlace tail.

And Jo loved him loads, all the way down the back of the sofa

and up the sleeves of her shirt

and round her neck

and into the pocket where she kept his sunflower seeds.

*But he wasn't the same as a dog.*

Her parents' eyes went up to the skies.

'There just isn't the space.'

'We haven't the room.'

'No,' said her father

and 'No,' said her mum.

'Why don't you go and play with next door's rabbit?'

Pleeease!

So Jo played with next door's big, lickety-hop, one ear up and one ear flopped white rabbit (and the little black guinea pig who kept it company).

And she loved them both all over the garden and through the muddy flowerbeds and across the clean kitchen floor and back to their hutch.

*But they weren't the same as a dog.*

Her parents sighed,

shook their heads from side to side.

'Dogs cost too much to keep.'

'And there's all that food.'

So 'No!' said her mother and 'No!' said her dad.

'But if you really, really must … we could get a cat …

As long as it's one of those small tidy ones!'

So they got a kitten with long fluffy fur, that purred like a motorbike, snuggled like a bear

and climbed the curtains whenever it could.
And Jo loved that kitten from waking-up to bedtime all day and every day. But …

… *it still wasn't the same as a dog.*

'Don't even suggest it.'

'This isn't the time.'

'No!' said her father and 'No!' said her mum.

'Because ...' and they looked very pleased with themselves ...

'We're going to have something much more exciting than a dog.

We're going to have ...

Pleeease!

a Baby!'

*Well, how about that!*

Jo's mum had the baby.
He was all round and gurgly.
He cuddled and cooed
and he sucked and he snoozed
and Jo loved that baby (mostly)

loads and loads and loads
and all the way to the end of time …

*But he wasn't the same as a dog.*

Her parents' sighs were multiplied.
'We live in the city, it wouldn't be fair on a dog,
all those lorries and buses and cars.'
'And who'd take it for walks?'
'A dog would be sad.'
'No no,' said her mother
and 'No,' said her dad.

So Jo got some stick insects instead.

She brought the school rabbits home for the holidays,
borrowed a budgerigar from up the road,

helped a hamster that needed a home,

collected ants, trawled for tadpoles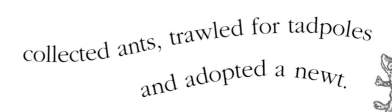
and adopted a newt.

And her parents scarcely even
noticed because they were much
too busy looking after the baby.

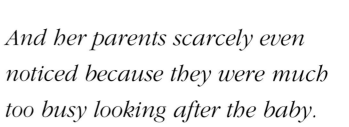

Well, the baby gurgled and the baby grew.
He laughed and he crawled and he learned how to

open rabbit hutch doors
and pull things off shelves
and smear food and gloop
all over himself
and everything else.

'Do you know what we need?' said Jo
(who still wanted a dog
more than anything else
in the whole wide world).
'We need a ...'

'Oh...'

'We may need a cleaner,

we may need a nanny.

'NO!'
said her father.

'No No No!'
said her mum.

We may need a cook

and lots more money,

a bigger house,

a good night's sleep,

but what we do NOT need is ...'

But just then there was a ring at the front doorbell
and there was Far-Away-Grandma
standing on the doorstep
with two big suitcases and a cardboard box!

'I thought it was about time I gave you
some help with that baby,' said Grandma.
'So here I am
and I've brought something especially for Jo,' she smiled,
pointing at the box.

So Jo sat down and undid the knots.
She pulled off the string, opened the flaps … And …

Woof! Woof!

tweet!

Quick as a flash, straight out of the top, jumped a bundle of fur that couldn't be stopped ...

It cleaned the baby from head to toe, wagged its tail and nuzzled at Jo ...

meow!

... it barked and it panted and bounced and then
it chased the rabbits back to their pen,
the cats to their cushions, the mice to their run.

... and Jo took one look at that bundle of fur
and loved it more than anything else in the whole wide world.

As for her parents,
they were so surprised that they sat down
for the first time for as long as they could remember
while Grandma put the kettle on for a nice cup of tea.

Aaaw! said her mother.

Aaah! said her dad.

# Bog Gog DOG!

chirped the baby ...

*And that was that!*